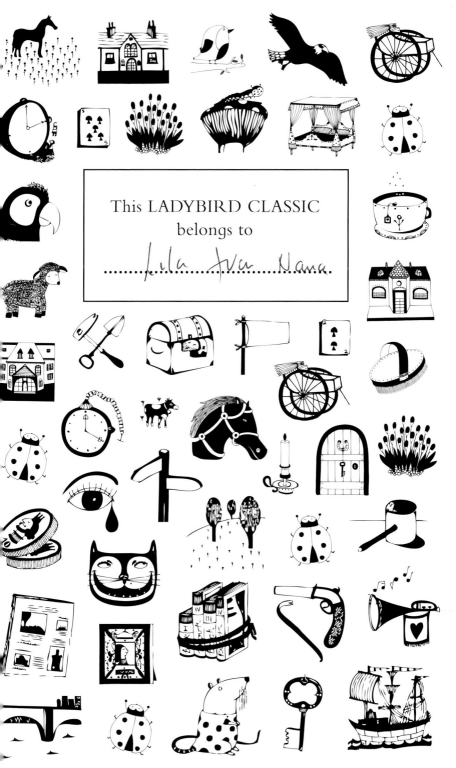

This LADYBIRD CLASSIC
belongs to

..........Lula Iva Nana.

A History of the Author

Edith Nesbit was born in 1858 and was one of the most popular and best-loved children's authors of the twentieth century. Her stories are known for combining realistic, everyday situations with magical events and fantasy.

Chapter illustrations by Valeria Valenza

A catalogue record for this book is available from the British Library

Published by Ladybird Books Ltd
80 Strand London WC2R 0RL
A Penguin Company

006

ISBN: 978-0-723-27086-7

Printed in China

LADYBIRD CLASSICS

The Railway Children

by E. Nesbit

Retold by Joan Collins
Illustrated by Silvana di Marcello

Contents

CHAPTER ONE

The Beginning of Things

THEY WERE NOT railway children to begin with. They lived near London, with their father and mother, in a red brick villa with coloured glass in the front door and lots of white paint. The only times they travelled by train were to go to the zoo or Madame Tussaud's.

There were three of them. Roberta, the eldest (whom everyone called "Bobbie") was perhaps her mother's secret favourite. Peter wanted to be an engineer. Phyllis meant well, but sometimes things seemed to go wrong for her.

They had a dog called James, and a mother who read to them, helped with their homework and wrote funny poems for their birthdays. Their father was perfect – never cross, never unfair, and always ready for fun. They were perfectly happy until, one day, a dreadful change came into their lives.

Late one evening, two men called to see their father, who was busy mending a toy railway engine for Peter. Then a taxi was ordered and Father went away in it. Their mother looked upset and was as white as a sheet. She asked the children just to be good and not to ask questions.

The children wanted to help, but they did not quite know how. Bobbie realized that something serious was making her mother miserable.

'I say,' said Phyllis to Bobbie, 'you used to say it was so dull – nothing happening like in books. Now something *has* happened!'

'I never wanted things to happen to make Mother unhappy,' Bobbie replied. 'Everything's perfectly horrid.'

Everything continued to be perfectly horrid for some weeks. Then they were told that their father, who worked for the government, had gone away on business and might be away on business for a long time.

Mother said, 'Don't worry! It'll all come right in the end!'

She told them they were going away to live in a little white house in the country. All the useful household things were packed up to be taken there in a van.

'We've got to play at being poor for a bit,' she said.

They all went down by train. When they arrived, they stood on the draughty platform and watched the rear lights of the guard's van disappear into the darkness.

They did not guess then how they would grow to love the railway, and how soon it would become the centre of their new life. It was a long, dark, muddy walk from the station to their new home. The rough country road led through a gate in the fields to a dark lumpish thing Mother said was the house, *Three Chimneys.*

There were no lights and the front door was locked. The carter, who brought their luggage, found the key under the doorstep, and lit a candle for them. They could hear a rustling and scampering in the walls.

'What's that noise?' asked the girls.

'Only the rats,' said the carter, going out. As the door shut after him, the draught blew out the candle.

'I wish we'd never come!' wailed Phyllis.

'*Only the rats!*' said Peter in the dark.

CHAPTER TWO

Peter's
Coal Mine

'WHAT FUN!' said Mother. 'This will be quite an adventure!'

A neighbour was supposed to have left them some supper, but they could not find any food. Mother found a small amount in one of the packing cases from home, so they had a picnic meal in the kitchen.

The next morning, the children woke early, and crept down, mousy quiet, to get everything ready for breakfast before Mother woke up.

They washed under the spout of the pump in the yard.

'It's much more fun than basin washing!' said Bobbie. 'How sparkly the weeds are!'

They lit the fire, put the kettle on, and laid the table. Then they went to explore.

The house stood in a field, on a hilly slope. Down below, they could see the line of the railway, and the black yawning mouth of a tunnel. The station was out of sight. There was a bridge with tall arches running across one end of the valley.

They all sat down on a flat stone in the grass to watch for trains. Mother found them, at eight o'clock, asleep in a contented, sun-warmed bunch.

By that time, the fire had burned out and the kettle had boiled dry. But Mother had found their supper laid in another

room, so they had it for breakfast – cold roast beef, bread and butter, cheese, and apple pie.

All the unpacking was done by late afternoon, and Mother went to lie down. So the children set off for the railway.

They slid down the short, smooth turf slope. The way ended in a steep run and a wooden fence, and there was the railway, with shining metal rails, telegraph wires, posts and signals.

Suddenly there was a rumbling sound, and a train rushed out of the tunnel with a shriek and a snort, and slid noisily past them. The stones between the lines jumped and rattled.

'Oh!' said Bobbie. 'It was like a great dragon passing by!'

'I never thought we should ever get so near to a train as this!' gasped Peter.

'I wonder if it's going to London,' said Bobbie. 'That's where Father is!'

'Let's go to the station and find out,' said Peter.

There were a great many crossing lines at the station. Some were just sidings with trucks standing in them. In one of these there was a great heap of coal, with a line of whitewash at the top.

The porter came out and told them that the white mark was to show how much coal was there, so that he would know if any had been 'nicked'.

'So don't you go off with none in your pockets, young gentleman!' (Peter was to remember this warning later.)

The children quickly settled down to their new life in the country. They got used to being without Father, though they did not forget him. Their mother wrote stories and sent them away to editors. Sometimes they came back, but sometimes a sensible editor kept one, and then they had halfpenny buns for tea.

Mother often reminded them that they were poor now. On a cold day in June, they asked for a fire and she said, 'Coal is so dear! Have a good romp in the attic – that will warm you up!'

This gave Peter an idea. 'If Mother asks what I'm doing, say I'm playing at mines,' he said.

'What sort of mines?'

'Coal mines! But don't tell, on pain of torture!'

Two nights later, he called the girls to help him, and bring the Roman Chariot. (This was an old pram they had found in a shed.) They guided it down the slope towards the station. Hidden in a hollow was a small heap of coal.

'This is from St Peter's Mine!' he said, and they hauled it home in the Chariot. Mrs Viney, their daily help, remarked how well the coal was holding out that week!

But one dreadful night the Station

Master caught Peter scrabbling around in the coal heap.

'I'm not a thief!' Peter insisted. 'I'm a coal miner!' Bobbie and Phyllis, who had been hiding behind a truck, came bravely out to join Peter.

'Why, it's a whole gang of you!' exclaimed the Station Master. 'The children from Three Chimneys! Don't you know it's wrong to steal? What made you do such a thing?'

Peter explained how his mother had said they were too poor to have a fire. He thought it wasn't wrong to take coal from the middle of the pile – it was like mining.

The Station Master promised to overlook it "this once". 'But remember, stealing is stealing, even if you call it mining! Now run along home!'

'You're a brick!' said Peter.

'You're a dear!' said Bobbie.

'You're a darling!' said Phyllis.

CHAPTER THREE

The Old Gentleman

THE CHILDREN COULD not keep away from the railway and the Station Master, who had forgiven them for the coal, said they could visit whenever they liked. Before long they had given the trains names. The 9.15 up to London was the *Green Dragon*. The midnight express, which sometimes woke them from their dreams, was the *Fearsome Fly by Night*.

They made a friend, a kind-faced old gentleman who travelled on the 9.15. He waved to them as they watched the *Green Dragon* tear out of its dark lair in the tunnel, and they waved back. They liked to think that perhaps he knew their father in London and would take their love to him.

The porter, whose name was Perks, told them all sorts of fascinating things about trains. You were only allowed to pull the communication cord if you were going to be murdered or something. An old lady had pulled it once because she thought it was the refreshment car bell and ordered a Bath bun when the guard came. Perks also told them about the different kinds of engines. Peter started to collect engine numbers in a notebook.

One day their mother was taken ill, and Peter had to fetch the doctor from the village. He said it was influenza, and gave her some medicine. He also said she should

have beef tea, brandy and all sorts of luxuries. The children were very worried.

'We've got to do something!' said Bobbie. 'Let's think hard.' At last they had an idea. They got a sheet and made a big notice that read:

"LOOK OUT AT THE STATION"

They fixed it up on the fence, and pointed at it when the train went by. Phyllis ran ahead to the station with a letter for the old gentleman. It told how ill their mother was and what they needed, and promised to repay him when they grew up. The old gentleman read it, smiled and put it in his pocket. Then he went on reading *The Times*.

That evening Perks came to their door with a big hamper. In it was everything they had asked for, and more – peaches, two chickens, port wine, red roses and a bottle of Eau-de-Cologne. There was also a letter from the old gentleman. He said it

was a pleasure to help, and their mother was not to be cross with them for asking.

A fortnight later, another notice went up:

"SHE IS NEARLY WELL, THANK YOU"
Mother was very angry at first, but she knew the children had only wanted to help.

'You must never, never ask strangers to give us things!' she said earnestly. 'But I must write to thank your old gentleman for his kindness.'

CHAPTER FOUR

Prisoners and Captives

ONE DAY, MOTHER went to Maidbridge, the nearest town, to post some letters. The children went to meet her train, and as they were early, they played games in the General Waiting Room.

When the London train came in, the children went to talk to their friend, the engine driver. They were surprised to see a crowd on the platform, around a man with long hair and wild eyes. He was trembling and looked ill, and he was talking in a foreign language that nobody could understand. Peter asked him, 'Parlay voo Frongsay?'

The man poured out a flood of words that Peter knew were French, though he did not understand them. The children had been taught French at school. How they wished they had learned it! But their mother could speak French, and she would be on the next train.

Bobbie begged the Station Master not to frighten the man. 'His eyes look like a fox's in a trap!'

'I think I ought to send for the police,' said the Station Master.

Just then Mother's train came in. She spoke to the stranger in French, and he replied excitedly. 'It's all right,' she said. 'He's Russian, and he's lost his ticket. I'm going to take him home with me and I'll tell you

more in the morning. He's a great man in his own country. He writes books – beautiful books – I've read some of them.'

When they got home, Mother took some of Father's clothes out of a trunk for the man. Bobbie felt terrible and asked if Father was dead.

Mother gave her a hug. 'Daddy is quite well, and he will come back to us some day, darling.'

That night Mother told them about the Russian gentleman. He had written a book about the poor people in Russia in the time of the Tsar and how the rich people ought to help them. Because of this, he was put in prison and then sent to Siberia, where he was very badly treated.

'How did he get away?' the children asked.

Mother explained that prisoners were sent as soldiers to war, and he had deserted. He had come to England, to

look for his wife and children, but lost
his train ticket and got out at the
wrong station.

'Do you think he'll find his family?'

'I hope and pray so,' said Mother.

Then, after a pause, she said, 'Dears,
when you say your prayers, ask God
to pity all prisoners and captives.'

'To pity,' Bobbie repeated slowly,
'all prisoners and captives. Is that right?'

CHAPTER FIVE

Saviours of
the Train

THE RUSSIAN GENTLEMAN was
soon well enough to sit out in the garden.
Mother wrote to Members of Parliament
and other people who she thought might
know where his family could be. The
children could not talk with him, but they
showed their friendship by smiling and
bringing him flowers.

One day they had the idea of fetching

him wild cherries that grew along the cliff by the mouth of the tunnel. When they got to the top of the cutting, they looked down to where the railway lines lay.

It was like a mountain gorge, with bushes and trees overhanging the cutting. A narrow 'ladder' of wooden steps led down to the line, with a swing gate at the top. They were almost at the gate when Bobbie suddenly said, 'Hush! Stop! What's that?'

"That" was a sort of rustling, whispering sound. It stopped then started again, louder and more like a rumbling. 'Look at that tree!' cried Peter.

A tree with grey leaves and white flowers seemed to be moving, shivering and walking down the slope. Then all the trees seemed to be sliding towards the railway line.

'What is it? I don't like it!' cried Phyllis. 'Let's go home!'

'It's all coming down,' said Peter. As he

spoke, the great rock on which the trees grew leaned slowly forward. The trees stood still and shivered. Then rock, grass, trees and bushes slipped right away from the face of the cutting and fell on the line with a mighty crash. A cloud of dust came up.

'It's right across the down line!' said Phyllis.

'The 11.29's due!' said Peter. 'We must let them know at the station, or there'll be a frightful accident!'

'There's not enough time,' said Bobbie. 'What can we do? We ought to wave a red flag!'

The girls were wearing red flannel petticoats. They hurriedly took them off and ripped them to pieces, so that they had six flags. Peter made flagpoles from saplings and made holes to stick them through. Then they stood ready, each with two flags, waiting for the train.

Bobbie thought that no one would

notice the silly little flags, and everyone would be killed. Then came the distant rumble and hum of the metals, and a puff of white smoke far away.

'Stand firm,' said Peter, 'and wave like mad!'

'It's no good, they won't see us!' said Bobbie.

The train came faster and faster, and Bobbie ran forward.

'Keep off the line!' said Peter fiercely.

'Not yet! Not yet!' cried Bobbie, and waved her flags right over the line. The front of the engine looked enormous. Its voice was loud and harsh.

'Oh stop, stop, stop!' cried Bobbie. The engine must have heard her, for it slackened speed swiftly and stopped dead. Bobbie still waved her flags, as Peter ran to meet the engine driver. Then she collapsed across the line.

'Gone off in a faint, poor little girl,' said

the engine driver, 'and no wonder!'

They took her back to the station in the train, and she gradually came to life and began to cry.

At the station they were cheered and praised like heroes, and their ears got very red.

'Let's go home,' said Bobbie, thinking what might have happened to the people.

'It was us that saved them!' said Peter.

'We never got any cherries, did we?' said Bobbie. The others thought her rather heartless.

CHAPTER SIX

For Valour

THERE IS A good deal about Roberta
in this story. That is because there are all
sorts of things about her that I love.

   She was anxious to make other people
happy. And she could keep a secret. She
never said anything that would let her
mother know how much she wondered
what she was unhappy about. That was
not as easy as you might think.

Another thing about Roberta was that she tried to help people. She wanted to help the Russian gentleman to find his wife and child. One day, she got her chance.

The railway decided to make a presentation of three gold watches to the children, for their brave action in saving the train. There was a little ceremony at the station, and Peter made a modest speech, saying, 'What we did wasn't anything really – at least, it was awfully exciting, and thank you all very much!'

The old gentleman was there, and Bobbie asked to speak to him in private. She told him all about the Russian – 'Mr Sczcepansky – you call it Shepansky.' The old gentleman had heard of him, and had read his book. 'So your mother took him in,' he said. 'She must be a very good woman.'

Just then Phyllis came in, carrying a tin can and a thick slice of bread and butter

that Perks had given her. 'Afternoon tea!'
she announced.

Ten days later, the old gentleman came
through the fields to see the children.

'Good news!' he said. 'I've found your
Russian's wife and child!'

Bobbie raced ahead to be the first
home with the news. Mother's face lit up,
and she spoke a few French words to the
Russian. He sprang up with a cry of joy,
and gratefully kissed Mother's hand. Then
he sank into his chair, covered his face
with his hands, and sobbed.

Bobbie crept away. She did not want
to see the others just then. When she came
back, the old gentleman gave the three
children a big box of chocolates each.

The Russian's few belongings were
packed, and they all saw him off at the
station. As they walked home, Mother
seemed very tired. Phyllis was talking
about the Russian's baby, and how it must

have grown since he saw it last. 'I wonder if Father will think I've grown!' she said.

Bobbie said, 'Come on, Phil, I'll race you to the gate!'

You know why Bobbie did that. But Mother only thought Bobbie was tired of walking slowly. Even mothers, who love you better than anyone else, don't always understand everything.

CHAPTER SEVEN

The Terrible Secret

ONE DAY, WHEN Mother was
writing, Bobbie brought her some tea.
Mother said, 'Bobbie, you children aren't
forgetting Father, are you? You never talk
about him now.'

'Yes, we do, when we're by ourselves.
We thought it made you unhappy to
speak about him.'

'No, Bobbie dear,' said Mother, putting

her arm around her. 'Father and I have had a great sorrow – worse than you could ever think of – but it would be much worse if you were to forget him!'

'I promised not to ask questions,' Bobbie said in a small voice, 'but will the trouble last always?'

'No!' said Mother. 'The worst will be over when Father comes home to us, I promise.'

The next day, Peter fell over a rake in the garden and hurt his foot. He had to stay indoors, so Bobbie went down to ask Perks for any magazines people had left on the train. Perks wrapped them up in a newspaper for her to carry.

She had to wait at the level crossing for a train to pass, so she rested the parcel on the top of the gate and glanced at the printing on the paper.

Suddenly she clutched the parcel – it seemed like a horrible dream. She read on, but the bottom of the column was torn off. As soon as she got home, she ran to her room and locked the door. Then she undid the parcel, and read the column again. Her face was burning, but her hands felt icy cold. 'So now I know!' she whispered.

What she had read was headed, "End of the Trial. Sentence." The man who had been tried was her father. The verdict was "Guilty". The sentence was "Five Years' Penal Servitude".

'Oh Daddy!' she whispered. 'It's not true! I don't believe it! You never did it! Never, never!'

There was a hammering on the door.

'It's me,' said Phyllis. 'Tea's ready. Come along down!'

Bobbie struggled through tea, pretending she had a headache. Then she went up to her mother.

She did not know what to say.

At first she just cried bitterly, while her mother held her close. Then at last she pulled out the piece of newspaper and pointed to her father's name.

'Oh, Bobbie!' Mother cried. 'You don't believe Daddy did it, do you?'

'No!' Bobbie almost shouted.

'That's right. It's not true. They've shut him up in prison, but he's done nothing wrong.'

'Why didn't you tell me?'

'Are you going to tell the others?'

'No!'

'Why?'

'Because …' Bobbie started, then faltered.

'Exactly,' said Mother. 'So now you understand. We two must help each other to be brave.'

Mother told Bobbie how the men who had come to see Father that night had arrested him for selling State secrets. Letters had been found in Father's desk that made it look true. But there was a jealous man in

his office who wanted Father's job. Father thought he must have put the letters there, but he could not prove it.

'Couldn't we explain all that to somebody?'

'I've tried,' said Mother. 'Nobody will listen. All we can do is to be brave and patient, and pray.'

A week later Bobbie wrote a letter to her old gentleman, telling him everything, and sending the newspaper cutting:

'… Think if it was your Daddy, how you would feel. Oh do, do help me.

With love,
I remain, your affectionate little friend,
Roberta.'

CHAPTER EIGHT

The Hound in the Red Jersey

THE NEXT DAY the grammar school
boys were going on a paper chase. The
children went up to the top of the cutting
by the tunnel to watch.

In a little while the "hare" came by.
Carrying a shoulder bag of torn paper
to lay a trail, he ran off into the mouth
of the tunnel.

Then came the "hounds", following the

trail of torn paper down the wooden steps and into the tunnel. The last one wore a red jersey.

The children scrambled across the top to see them come out at the other end. It seemed a long time before the hare came panting out of the tunnel. After him came the hounds, in twos and threes, all very slow and tired.

'There's still one more to come,' said Peter, counting. 'The one in the red jersey.' They waited, but he did not come.

'Suppose he's had an accident! He might be lying there helpless in the path of an engine!' said Peter.

'Don't talk like a book!' said Bobbie. They set off into the tunnel. You had to walk on stepping stones and gravel, on a path that curved downwards from the metals to the wall. Slimy trickles of water ran down the sickly green bricks. As the tunnel gradually got darker, Peter lit a

candle he happened to have in his pocket.

Then they heard a humming sound along the wires by the track.

'It's a train!'

'Let me go back!' said Phyllis, frightened.

'Don't be a coward! You're quite safe!' said Bobbie. Peter pushed them into a damp, dark recess in the wall.

The train roared towards them, its dragon eyes of fire growing brighter. And then, with a rush and a roar and a rattle, with a smell of smoke and a blast of hot air, the train hurtled by, clanging and jangling and echoing in the arched roof.

'Oh!' said the children all together, in a whisper.

'Suppose the boy with the red jersey was in the way of the train!' said Phyllis.

'We've got to go and see,' said Peter.

About a hundred and fifty yards on they saw a gleam of red. There, by the line, was the red-jerseyed hound, his back against

the wall, his arms limp and his eyes shut.

'Is he killed?' squeaked Phyllis.

'No, he's only fainted,' said Peter. He rubbed the boy's hands, and Phyllis splashed milk from the picnic bottle on his forehead.

Bobbie said, 'Oh look up, speak to me. For my sake, speak!' (Which was what people always said in books when somebody fainted.)

CHAPTER NINE

What Bobbie Brought Home

AT LAST THE boy sighed, opened his eyes and said in a very small voice, 'Chuck it!'

'Fear not,' said Peter, 'you are in the hands of friends!'

'I believe I've broken my leg,' groaned the boy. 'I tripped on these wires. How did you get here?'

'We saw you hadn't come out of the

tunnel, so we came in to look for you. We're a rescue party!' said Peter proudly.

'You've got some pluck!' the boy said, and shut his eyes again.

Peter and Phyllis set off to fetch help. Bobbie chose to stay with the 'hound' in the dark. It seemed a long time, and they held hands for comfort. Bobbie managed somehow to cut the laces on his boot and ease the swollen leg. Then men from a nearby farm came with a hurdle, and carried the hound to *Three Chimneys*.

Their mother thought they had brought a dog home – till she saw the hound was only a boy.

'Couldn't we keep him till he's better, Mother?' begged Peter. 'It'd be ripping to have another chap to talk to!'

'We'll see,' said Mother. It turned out that Jim (that was the hound's name) had no mother of his own and lived with his grandfather. His school was closing for the

holidays. So Mother thought it could be arranged.

You will never guess who Jim's grandfather turned out to be.

Yes, it was the old gentleman!

When he found out what Mother had done, he knew that she could not afford it, so he made Mother "Matron of Three Chimneys Hospital", with a proper salary. He sent lots of food and two of his own servants to help with the work.

Jim and Peter became great friends. But Jim never forgot how kind Bobbie had been to him in the tunnel, and how brave she had been.

When Jim's grandfather came, he spoke to Roberta about her letter.

'When I first read your father's case in the paper, I had my doubts,' he said. 'And since I've known who you were, I've been trying to find out things. I haven't done much yet, but I have hopes! But keep our

secret a little longer. It wouldn't do to upset your mother with a false hope.'

Whether it was a false hope or not, it lit up Bobbie's face like a candle in a Japanese lantern.

CHAPTER TEN

The End

JIM TAUGHT PETER to play chess
and dominoes, and his leg got better
and better.

Life at *Three Chimneys* was pleasant,
but also rather dull. Having servants to
do everything made it seem a long time
since that first morning when they had
burned the bottom out of the kettle. They
hardly seemed railway children any more,

because they spent most of their time
at home.

'Perhaps something wonderful will
happen,' said Peter one afternoon.

And something wonderful did happen,
just four days later.

It was September now, and the turf on
the slope was dry and crisp. It had been
a long time since the children had waved
to the 9.15 and sent their love to Father by
it. They decided that this morning was the
perfect time to start again.

'Hurry,' said Peter, 'or we shall miss it!'
Phyllis stumbled over her bootlace as they
all ran, waving and shouting, 'Take our
love to Father!'

The old gentleman waved from his
carriage window. He always waved. But
today everybody waved – handkerchiefs,
papers and hands from every window!

'WELL!' the children all said.

'I thought the old gentleman was trying

to tell us something with his newspaper,' said Bobbie.

'Tell us what?' asked Peter.

'I don't know, but I feel awfully funny, as if something were going to happen.'

Later that morning, Bobbie decided to go for a walk down to the station. On her way, several of the villagers greeted her.

The old lady from the Post Office gave her a kiss and a hug and said, 'God bless you, dear!'

The blacksmith said, 'Good morning, Missie! I wish you joy, that I do.'

The Station Master shook her hand warmly and said, 'The 11.54's a bit late.'

Even the station cat gave Bobbie a special purr.

Finally Perks came out, holding a newspaper. 'One I must have, Miss, on a day like this!' he said, and kissed her cheek.

'A day like what?' asked Bobbie, but before he could answer, the 11.54 steamed

into the station.

Of course, you know what was going to happen, but Bobbie was not so clever. She felt confused and expectant, without knowing what she expected.

Only three people got out of the 11.54. A farmer's wife with a basket of live chicks. A lady with several brown paper parcels. And a third…?

'Oh, my Daddy, my Daddy!' That scream went like a knife into the hearts of everyone there.

People put their heads out to see a tall, thin, pale man, and a little girl clinging to him with arms and legs, while his arms went tightly around her.

As they went up the road, her father said, 'You must go in by yourself, Bobbie, and tell Mother quietly. It's all right. They've caught the man who did it. Everyone knows it wasn't your Daddy.'

'We always knew it wasn't!' said Bobbie.

'Me and Mother and our old gentleman!'

So Bobbie went in to tell Mother that the sorrow was over, and Father had come home. Father waited in the garden, looking at the flowers, the first he had seen for a long time.

Then the door opened. Bobbie called, 'Come in, Daddy! Come in!'

I think we will not follow him. It is best for us to go quietly away and take a last look at the white house where no one else is needed now.

Collect more fantastic
LADYBIRD 🐞 CLASSICS

Alice in Wonderland

9781409311232

Oliver Twist

9781409311256

Treasure Island

9781409311287

BLACK BEAUTY

9781409311249

GULLIVER'S Travels

9781409311270

The Secret Garden

9781409311263

A Christmas Carol

9781409312215

Peter Pan

9781409312222

The Three Musketeers

9781409313557

THE WIND IN THE WILLOWS

9781409313564

Heidi

9781409313571

The Jungle Book

9781409313588

The Railway Children

9780723270867

Little Women

9780723270874